IN SEARCH OF HOPE

From the Book

"Despair, Hope, Salvation"

By

Alford Pelton

About the Author

The author of this book is just like everyone else: *Made of Flesh and Blood, Born of a Woman, Created from Dust, Created in the Image of God, Fallen from Grace; and yet, so loved by God that He sent His only begotten Son that we can again be redeemed unto Him by His grace.* We can be thankful that even though we are but dust, we are precious dust. Psalm 103:14, speaking of God's great love and compassion for us states; ***"For He knows our frame; and remembers that we are dust"***. Let us rejoice and remember that even as dust, Ephesians 2:9 states that ***"we are God's workmanship, created in Christ Jesus for good works, which God prepared beforehand that we should walk in them"***. I pray that the work He has given me do, and that He has given us all to do, will be done according to His will, and His good pleasure.

My greatest love is for God, family, friends, people and writing. I published my first two books in 1973. Over the years, I maintained my love for God, family, friends and people; but I became so busy trying to make a living until I found little time for writing, but never lost my love for writing. It is my hope that everyone who reads this book will enjoy reading it as much as I loved writing it.

About the Book

This book is an excerpt taken from the book *"Despair, Hope, Salvation"*; which is a book based on the tribulations, troubles, trials and triumphs of life. We find that life can be a stairway taking us up or down, and we get to choose which direction we will travel. We can start in Despair and continue to travel in a direction that will take us deeper into the depths of doubt and darkness; or we can choose to go from Despair into the light of Hope. Romans 8:24-25 states; *"For we are saved by hope: but hope that is seen is not hope; for why should one still hope for what he sees? But if we hope for what we do not see, we eagerly wait for it with perseverance"*. Hebrews 11:1 also speaks to this truth: *"Now faith is the substance of things hoped for, the evidence of things not seen"*.

The first portion of this book contains poems concerning **Hope, Love, Life** a desire for the **Peace** and **Joy** that comes from **Hope**. The second portion of the book contains assays that speak of a search for **Hope** and **Identity**.

It is my hope that all who read this book will not only find some measure of **Hope**, but will go beyond the place of **Hope** to the place of **Peace** and **Joy** that God has prepared for us all. Proverbs 13:12 states; *"Hope deferred makes the heart sick: but when the desire comes, it is a tree of life"*. Take heart in knowing that *hope deferred does not mean hope denied*. We should always remain hopeful, searching for the *"tree of life"*.

But remember that this book is not about finding hope; it is merely about searching for hope. Never forget that **True Hope** can only be found in one book – *the Book of Truth, the Book of Hope, the Book of Faith, the Book of Life* – the Bible.

Table of Contents

Hope

When life is filled with deep despair,
As there is no one to care
  That your hopes have faded away,
  As does night with the arrival of day;
And your burdens are too heavy to bear.

When hope seeps as do grains of sand....
Through your fingers when held in your hand;
  Seep slowly, to return no more
  As you hold them tighter than before,
And watch them fall slowly upon the land.

Hope, fade not; hope, go not away.
Please stay within my reach for one more day.
  When I call, please be there
  To prevent me from feeling despair
That your comfort has gone astray.

When hope passes as the hands of time – slowly by;
When that time ends, as must I;
  Within my heart is this constant prayer,
  Let not my hope turn to despair
When it comes my time to die.

Simple Pleasures Are the Best

The sparkle in eyes that are bright; a whole-hearted grin,
The sound of a welcomed hello; the company of a relative or friend:
The tender touch of a loving hand; a warm and loving smile:
It is the simple pleasures that make us know life is worthwhile.

The look of summer, the smell of spring,
The beautiful sound of birds that sing;
A hard day of work, a long night of leisure,
Oh! How we long for life's simple pleasures.

A soft evening breeze; a fresh spring rain,
Memories of someone dear, that will always remain.
A boat at sail on a clear blue sea,
So sweet will such pleasures remain to me.

To run and play along the beach,
To meet your love, with arms outreached.
Knowing your love will always be true,
Yes, my greatest pleasure is being with you.

Sweet Dreams

Dreams …., those ever-elastic stretches of time
That comes before us, as the body unwinds:
And upon our memories are left the many signs
As to wonderful dreams, our body resigns.

Dreams, beautiful dreams that come as our mind is at peace,
Our many tensions and anxieties, they do release:
And our troubles will tend to cease,
As dreams put our bodies at ease:

Reality is sweet, but even sweeter are dreams;
For life isn't what it is, but merely what it seems.
In reality we are judged, but we may be redeemed
When our bodies return to their many sweet dreams:

The many moods of love

To many, love is like water flowing from a faucet;
  (To be turned on and off by all who wish to drink the sweet liquid of life;)
To some, it is like water drawn from a well,
  (To be shared by all who wish to pull the rope of its refreshing ecstasy)
To others, it is like water in a bucket;
  (To be shared by the few who are able to dip into it)
To others, still, it is like water in a glass;
  (To be enjoyed by only one, and to be shared with no other)
Though each of these moods of love is different in its own way,
    They all are quite similar:
Each mood of love is to be shared, whether with one, or with many.
Each mood of love must eventually come to an end:
The faucet love will be turned off, to never be turned on again.
The well love will run dry, as all wells must.
The bucket love is limited in capacity, and will soon become empty.
The glass love will eventually be emptied and cast aside.
So, we see the many moods of love, each is as different from the other as is the characteristics of the human heart; and, as similar as the elements which makes us who we are.

A Letter to My Love

Dear love,

You asked me if I love you true;
I answered, *"Yes, I do"*.
Now, I ask the same question of you,
Can you say that you love me too?

If a thousand years should pass, and we both stay,
Though my skin be wrinkled and my hair is grey;
Will you love me more with the passing of each day?
Or, will you find pleasure with others, and go on your merry way?

Do you love me for who I am, or, for who you want me to be?
When you look into my eyes, what do you really see?
Do you see me, or just a reflection of me?
If I remain as I am, will your love remain at its same degree?

When I am dead, and return as clover,
When all my beauty you will discover;
Will you continue to be my lover?
Will you love me always, and forever?

My Lover's Answer

To my love,

You asked me if I love you true.
My answer is, *"I love only you"*.
Need you ask this question of me?
When my love, you so clearly see:

You asked if I will love you when we have both grown old.
As age turns coal to diamond, so shall it turn our love to gold.
As each day passes and go,
May our love be greater than the day before.

Yes, I love you for who you are, and everything you will be.
Just always be yourself, and nothing else matters to me.
Whatever the future holds for you,
My love will remain just as true.

And if you should die before I do,
My tears will fall as the morning dew.
And, until we both be together again,
My love for you will always remain.

Comparison of Beauty

Beautiful is a flower that blooms in May
Beautiful is the sun on a clear blue day
Beautiful is the dawn in the morning dew
But never so beautiful, my love, as you

Beautiful are the trees that bud in spring
Beautiful is the sound as a nightingale sings
Beautiful is the mink, the most beautiful of furs
But never can its beauty be compared to yours

Beautiful is music, so sweet to the ear
Beautiful is all that we hold so dear
Beautiful is beauty, a sight for all to view,
But even beauty blushes, my love, at the sight of you

God's Gift

God drew dirt from the ground and created man:
He gave him both feet and hands.
God gave him eyes with which to see,
And put in his heart a longing to be free.

God gave man a companion to always be at hand:
He called his companion by the name of woman.
God put them together, and commanded them to love;
And protected them from heaven above.

God supplied them with food to eat:
And gave them protection from head to feet.
God knew that they must someday die;
He, therefore, blessed them to multiply.

God supplied man with his every need
And gave him power to do noble deeds.
God gave man the gift of knowledge; and the will to be free:
But god's greatest gift was you, *His gift to me.*

Our Lives Are Like a Day

Our lives are like unto a day.
We come as sunlight…
Arising at dawn in the early morn…
Bright and full of energy:
We slowly rise to the pinnacle of daylight,
Too old to be called youthful morning,
And yet, not ready to be called the old age of evening.
From here, we begin our decline,
Losing the intensity we once possessed
Until, we come to the dusky reaches of evening:
We then go from twilight to the darkness of night;
There, to rest the eternal rest…
No more mornings to praise.
No more noondays to honor.
No more evenings to dread.

Our Body Is a Clock

Our body is but a clock;
Our mind is the controlling device…
Our heart, slowly ticking, is the passing of time.
From our earliest beginnings, we are wind up;
And placed in us are many preset alarms.
We hurt, we bleed, we cry,
Each alarm rings;
Yet, time moves on.
But, our *hour* is marked:
For many of us, life is as the stopwatch;
    (Though we run a good race, the end comes quickly.)
For others, life is as the old grandfather clock hanging on the wall;
    (The years pass slowly, as time gradually ticks away.)
But for each life, there is this certainty…
Our timing mechanism must someday end,
As our hands no longer revolve around the face of the clock,
And we become but the broken time of yesterday…
Discarded, and replaced by a new timepiece.

Silence

Silence is the greatest speaker of all:
It may cause nations to rise, or kingdoms to fall.
The answers for many questions may be given by only a hint,
But many more answers are given by silence, which always gives
consent.

Let not your words fall upon a deaf ear.
Let your thoughts be known by the fruit you bear.
Let all know your feelings by the things you do;
Words can be deceiving, but your actions are true.

Listen to the moon riding through the night:
You can't hear it with your ears; you must listen with your sight.
Yes, the moon speaks for all to hear;
Its words are beautiful to the eyes, but silent to the ear.

Two hearts meet… words need not be said,
Love dwells in silence; which, to hatred is dead.
If words were spoken, they could be wrong…
Who knows what evil controls the mind and the tongue?

Remember, before you speak those words of love,
Say them in a way that can be proved…
Say them from the heart, where truth plants the seed,
After all is said and done, silence is what we need.

Words Not Spoken

Words not spoken are heard the most;
Words spoken are too soon spent…
Let not your words give host,
For silence gives consent.

There is solitude in silence,
One need not be bored…
When we know the beauty whence,
Comes from unspoken words.

The eyes speak in a silent tone,
They speak and they are heard:
Within them is the beauty alone,
Of the many unspoken words.

So, speak not of love,
Talk not 'till you are awoken;
It only goes to prove that
The sweetest words are those which are yet unspoken.

The Tongue

Sharp is the pain
When lies are flung,
Merely the size of a grain of sand
From an evil tongue.
Though small a lie may be,
It can soon increase…
It need not be big for all to see;
The biggest lies are seen the least.
Speaker of truth, and speaker of lies;
Sayer of words; singer of songs:
The greatest power on earth cannot defy
The almighty weapon… the tongue.

No Limit

I threw a rock upon the ground;
When I went to retrieve it,
    There, two did I find.

I cast my line into the sea;
But instead of one fish,
    I did catch three.

I shot an arrow into the sky;
Instead of one bird,
    Four did fly.

I made a wish, and the fortunes were many;
Had I not made the wish,
    There wouldn't have been any.

From this, I've learned a great lesson
That we all should behold,
    Always let your aim, be greater than your goal.

An Impression

I helped a lady in distress;
And was I happy? Yes!
As I was about to swirl,
She said *"Thank you"*
And I knew,
I had left an impression on the world.

My Star

In the midst of a star covered sky,
One special star caught my eye.
It was a star far more beautiful than the rest;
To obtain it became my only quest.

It shined as the brilliance of the fairest sun;
It glowed as the light of a thousand moons:
It glittered with light, it glowed with fire,
To obtain this star became my sole desire.

Oh, star of mine, how beautiful you are.
Much more beautiful than the rest by far:
How close you are, and yet how far,
Oh, how I long to be where you are!

If

If I could prove that I don't love you;
If I could convince my heart that love isn't true:
If I could live and not love you,
Then, there would be no need for me to feel as I do.

If I could watch a thousand stars and not see your eyes;
If I could kneel beneath the moon and not behold your smile:
If you tell me you don't love me, and my heart doesn't cry;
Then, my heart would have no pain when you tell me goodbye.

If I could kiss each drop of rain, and not desire to kiss your lips so
sweet;
If my heart does not melt each time we meet:
If I could exist without you and my life still be complete,
Then, I could walk as a man, and not desire to spend eternity
kneeling at your feet.

If I could live my life and not think of you;
If I could depart from your love and not feel so blue:
If I could wake a thousand days, and never feel the morning's dew,
Then, I would have no need to love you as I truly do.

If I could be bathed in the warmth of the sun and not feel your love;
If I could hold you in my arms and not know the joy from above:
If I could hold you in my arms, and my love for you I could not
prove,
Then, I will weep no more when my love for you must be removed.

If I could open the door of life to depart;
And not think of you with all of my heart:
If my love for you should stop to never again restart,
Then, I shall have no need to cry when my love for you must part.

True Love Knows No Season

Enter not into that calendar of love my dear;
    For love there endures but twelve months of the year:
Enter not, and listen to my reason;
    True love, my dear, knows no season.

Will you love me my dear, just for the spring?
    Spring contains only March, April and May;
    Spring must end someday:
And I will fall as a dethroned king;
    Love me my love, tomorrow as today.

And what of summer, it too is short;
    It contains June, July and August:
    Must only these months, your love, I trust?
And afterwards, we take our seasonal part....
    No! Your love must remain – it must!

Then comes autumn, the season of decline;
    Autumn has September, October and November,
    Months you can easily forget to remember.
When your love is no longer mine,
    Let not our love become the remains of dying ember.

(Continued)

True Love Knows No Season

(Continued)

Alas! Now approaches winter – season of dread!
    In winter we find December, January and February;
    As do these months, will your love vary?
Will the passing of winter find our love dead?
    No: Let not our hearts grow cold and weary.

These four seasons to the calendar of the year;
    Twelve months in all
    For our love to rise or fall:
Must these months be filled with fear?
    That they separate us with a seasonal wall?

Enter not into that calendar of love my dear;
    For love there endures but part of the year:
Enter not, and listen to my reason;
    True love, my dear, knows no season.

A Tribute to Dr. King

(Continued)

From some distant hierarchy of mortal man,
There came a fighter for freedom throughout the land.
His weapon was words, his goal was peace;
He commanded an army which fought that all hatred may cease.

He spoke of love for all mankind,
But little of this love could he ever find.
When he spoke of this love, the words would echo in the ear;
They caused some to love, but many to fear.

Yes, he protested, but his protest was in peace:
He knew that if love could defeat evil, it would be victorious over
the beast.
His protest was such that the world could see;
As he commanded that all men become free.

He stormed the jails; he walked the street;
He marched until callouses were hardened on his feet.
But in his fight to set men free,
Quite often, fruitless would his struggle be.

Many times did his battles fail:
He was either beaten or thrown in jail.
But he never became discouraged, nor did he complain;
He always prepared his weapon to go to battle again.

With words as his weapon and truth as his shield;
He would always march forth to the battle field.
And though the laws of man condemned his fight;
He continually marched for freedom and right.

A Tribute to Dr. King

(Continued)

And though he died before the war was won,
He became a catalyst for others to carry on.
So, in all the world let freedom ring,
As a living tribute to Dr. King!

Truth and Reality

What is truth? What is reality? These are the two basic questions for which man seeks answers to every day of his life. In man's search for his true identity – *(for who he really is)*, these are the questions that he is really asking. He may ask himself, "What is the truth about my existence?" "Do I really exist, or am I merely an illusion of the mind?" And if so, "Whose mind has this illusion been cast into, to wander unknowingly; forever seeking the beginning to an identity which, in reality, has never really existed in the first place?"

Upon careful examination of myself, I soon learn that I am no illusion of the mind – that is, of course, of my own mind. I use my hands to examine my body, and I find flesh – *human flesh*. I use my mind to examine the inner me, and I find that I have human thoughts, human emotions, human needs and desires. But still, this does not confirm my identity. It does not really prove the existence of a being. I, therefore, must search even further. I now look in the mirror and see some image of a human form. I taste sugar; there is sweetness. I taste vinegar and sense that it is sour. I taste poison and sense that it is bitter. I find myself using all of the senses at man's disposal, and upon their uses, I find affirmative results. But now, the question before me is, can I use these positive results to draw some conclusion of my real existence? With regret and dismay, the only real answer I could give was "no". Why no, you may ask? The answer to this question is really quite simple. You see, if I am an illusion, why can't my mind also be an illusion: an illusion within an illusion. Then, my illusive hands would be examining the illusive flesh of its illusive body. My illusive mind would develop illusive thoughts along with illusive emotions. The image I see, or think I see, in the mirror would then become nothing more than a negative illusion – the negative counterpart to an existence that never really existed.

We now see that our search has led us to another part of life – that of negative illusions. What are negative illusions? These are really negative thoughts and realities. If we are to better understand what negative thoughts and realities are, we must first find the meaning of the supposedly positive truths and realities. Truth is the conformity with the facts or with reality, either as an idealized abstraction, or, in actual application to statements, or ideas. It is the quality of being in accordance with experience, facts; with actual existences. Reality is the quality of being real; factual. It is a condition of existing in actuality. Then, what are negative truths and negative realities? They are attempts to conform non-facts to experiences that never really existed. But why would one want to make a confirmation of nonfactual ideas with experiences that never really existed? Is it a sign of insanity? Is this person a victim of a psychopathic personality which, because of his emotional instability and lack of sound judgment, causes him to want to form substantiated existences from unsubstantiated ideas formed from delusive perceptions? No. these are not the reasons.

Truth and Reality

(Continued)

This attempted confirmation comes about as a result of some real experiences the person has had. But, because of man's ability to twist facts and truth to suit himself, he sometimes reshape the truth until it is no longer fact, but merely a negative truth formed from some factual existence.

Now, you may be asking, "but aren't these negative facts really lies?" No, he isn't really telling a lie. He is merely prevaricating. He confuses the issue to evade the truth. This distortion of the truth is not meant to deceive or to beguile those who may be connected with it; but rather, to delude them. The prevaricator merely wishes to fool someone – usually himself, or herself – so completely that they accept what is false as being true.

I am now forced into a state of wonderment, and maybe even a little bewilderment. For I am now forced to ask myself if I were to accept my previous positive results from my experiments to prove my identity – my human existence, would my acceptance be a prevarication? Do I wish so greatly to prove my identity and existence that I would be willing to accept the facts and then twist and distort them until they become a fabrication of what I think they should be?

Yes. I would be willing to commit the act of prevarication, and maybe many others, to prove my existence. For isn't it true that one of the basic human needs is that of belonging? But belonging to what? To a society whose mere continuance is based on a platform of shadows and things which cannot be substantiated, and placed within a realm of thought and illusions that do not exist? If this is the only companionable existence available, then yes; I would be willing to leave my isolated insubstantial existence to move and join those in a different society which is based on that same insubstantial existence. Just think of it. We will have formed, from one isolated illusion, an entire mass of conglomerated illusions. A society founded on illusions

24

and built on confusion. But with careful thought and consideration, I realized that this was not the society for me. After all, why should I leave one state of confusion, only to enter into another state of confusion? No, there has to be other answers to my dilemma. My true identity would have to be discovered by other means. I would have to make a more accurate examination in my search for the real truths and realities in life, separate these real truths and realities from those that are negative and illusive, and then, make more precise elucidations to clearly explain them and their relationships to the real and existent life.

Truth and Reality

But there is no positive means of severing substance from illusions, as we saw in our first investigation of attempting to ascertain some factual existence within society. There is no sure way to remove or separate two existences from each other, though one may be positive and the other one negative. The only boundary between these two existences is belief. It is rather hard to accept that something as important as one's identity is bordered upon such a narrow and flimsy source as that of belief. But it is our convictions that certain things are true, which sometimes make them true. We must believe that our state of human awareness makes us human. We must believe that human thoughts and deeds are capable of being performed only by the human element. It is therefore, when we perform such acts, we are human. If we accept all things as true when they are based on reasoning, or some sound source, then, they become true. They must be true, because of our convictions in them. We exist in a state of reality because we believe that such a state exists; and that we are a contributing force within it.

I now know my identity. I know the real me. Even though I was not able to base the foundation of such knowledge on suitable truths and substantiated realities, I was able to use the shaky grounds of belief to plant seeds of existence, and to cultivate these seeds to reap a harvest of sound conclusion as to my identity. I now know who I am, what I am, where I came from, and where I am going. I now know that I am what I believe myself to be. I came from a path of belief and I am traveling down a road of conviction. I know who I am because of my belief in myself, my trust in my fellow man, and my faith in God's word.

I have left many questions unanswered in my search for basic truths and realities: Questions to which the answers are quite vital if we are to continue our meager existences with some degree of certainty as to our identifiable characteristics. The major question that remains is;

'*are you sure of your identity*'? If not, maybe you can find the unknown answer to this question, and all of the other questions, in your search for *"Truth and Reality"*.

Emotion versus Logic

As human beings, we are often faced with two choices when making certain decisions; those of Logic or Emotion: When things happen in our lives, we may use use some pattern of logic in an attempt to insure an adequate or positive outcome to the situation. On other occasions, instead of using logic, we may find ourselves using our emotions, causing us to overreact, developing no definite pattern in our attempt to alleviate or end the situation. Or, maybe it would be more accurate to say that we are faced with the same situation, but two entirely different means of coming to some conclusion that will bring about a satisfactory end to the situation.

Let us look at the first choice, or method of accomplishment – that of emotions. But, we really can't call the use of emotions a choice, since we don't choose to use our emotions; but rather, they are an intense feeling forced upon us by some outward force or forces, causing us to react in some behavioral pattern *(over which we usually will not allow ourselves to control)*. Nor, can we wisely call it a method of accomplishment because the irrationality by which it is used usually allows much room for error in many cases; thereby, almost eliminating any chance of having a successful outcome.

To truly comprehend what emotional reactions entail, we must first look at the psychological and physical manifestations that usually bring about displays of emotionalism. We will find that in many cases, most of these emotions are detrimental to having a positive outcome. Let's look at the four most common emotions: **love, hate, fear** and **anger**. When we are confronted with either of these, we usually experience some strong physical excitement which leads us to irrational outbursts of our emotions. For **love**, we express passionate affection. For **hate**, we express a deep dislike or aversion. For **fear**, we express anxiety or agitation. And for **anger**, we express displeasure or indignation. It is true that these are perfectly normal human feelings. But abnormality exists when we express these feeling in excessive and destructive ways. Man's hasty arrival at such open expressions detours his ability to think, and, in so doing, deprives him of one of his greatest powers; the power to exercise his mental faculties, so as to form ideas, and arrive at a wise conclusion.

Now that we have seen the detrimental effects of emotions on human behavior, let's evaluate its association with human patterns of behavior. But, can we really associate human behavior with logic? Theory says the answer to this question is an overwhelming **"no"**! We must first consider that logic is a science. It deals with the study and explanation of facts about methods of reasoning.

Emotion versus Logic

(Continued)

Facts are used in relationship to each other, so as to arrive at a conclusion. It utilizes the process of thinking. Behaviorism, on the other hand, theorizes that man's actions are automatic responses to stimuli, and not dictated by consciousness. According to this theory, thinking is of little or no importance as far as human behavior is concerned, which eliminates reasoning completely. I hate to seem a nonconformist as far as theories are concerned, but in my studies of human nature and logic; and my close observations of fellow members of the human race, I am inclined to believe that logic must not only be associated with behaviorism, but is a large part of it. After all, when you are speaking of logic, it would be totally illogical to say man inevitably and invariably acts without giving any thought to the results of his actions.

If I were confronted with the question of "which acts do I prefer": Those arising from emotional outbursts, or, those which are the outcome of some degree of logic and reasoning; I would have to choose logic. After all, who in their right mind would not prefer being able to reason before acting on decisions that may affect their total wellbeing?

I consider myself to be a logical being. I resent any acts that are illogical and try to refrain myself from making them. Maybe, you are asking "why"? The answer to this question may well lie in an incident which occurred earlier in my life. It happened one Saturday evening on a beach. I was relaxing on the beach while my wife went for a ride in a canoe. I would have gone with her, but being the coward I am, and because of my great fear of drowning, I have developed an overpowering case of hydrophobia. As I looked up from my hammock, I noticed that the canoe had overturned. I saw my wife going down for the first time. My body erupted from a mass of potential inertia into a storm of dynamic kinetic energy. Without any thought of self-preservation, I jumped into the water and began stroking – one stroke, two strokes, three strokes.... I began kicking – one kick, two kicks, three kicks.... Amazingly, my bodily motions were forcing me in a forward direction. Yes, I was swimming. As I looked up, my wife was going down a second time. I began stroking even faster, and I noticed myself steadily approaching the "damsel in distress". As she was going under the third time, I instinctively reached out and I felt a great deal of weight in my arms. Yes, I had reached my goal. I was at her side. I had caught her around the waist and was struggling to reach a nearby boat. As my struggle carried me even nearer to the boat I was beginning to tire, but realizing the emergency at hand caused me to try even harder. My efforts finally brought me success. Yes, I had reaped the fruit of my labors. My wife was safe. But, as I used my last ounce of strength to bring my

Emotion versus Logic

wife to safety, the cold shock of reality dawned on me. A voice whispered from the back of my mind; *"fool, what are you doing here in this water? You know you can't swim"!* The whisper suddenly became a steady crescendo of vibrant shouts, with each shout becoming more frightening in its intensity. I grabbed the boat with both hands and held on for dear life. Those on the boat looked at me and saw the water on my face. They thought it was water from the ocean, but I knew better. I knew that the moisture on my face was really beads of sweat. Not sweat from exhaustion, but sweat from fear and anxiety. I feared dying. Never had I been so glad, as when I found myself safely aboard the boat.

Reminiscing over this incident, I often wonder whether I would have gone to my wife's rescue if I had first pondered the situation. Had I used logic, rather than letting my emotions control my actions, would I have been the hero I was after the occurrence? The answer is probably, "no". Yes, this is true. Had I thought first, I may not have gone to my wife's rescue, and she might have drowned. Now, maybe you ask why I feel logic should be exercised rather than letting emotions be the controlling factor in making decisions; especially when it was emotions instead of logic that caused me to save my wife's life? Maybe the answer to this question would have been found, had the outcome of the incident been different. Just suppose my attempt to be the rescuing hero had failed, and I had become the victim of the day. Then, what would have become of my emotional feeling? What would have become of any of my feelings? I would have just been another news story, and another name in the morgue; just another statistic in the nearest hall of records. Yes, the more I think about it, the more certain I am that, if the same situation were to occur once more, logic would triumph over emotions, and I would be forced to use the power of prayer, rather than physical exertion and risk of death as a means of rescue.

I have only tried to present to you my ideology of the concepts of logic and emotion; and their relationship to each other. Maybe you do not agree with my ideology. Therefore, it will be left up to you to do your own analytical research on the subject and arrive at a conclusion suitable to yourselves, as you ponder *"Emotion"* and *"Logic"*.

I

Pray

That All

Who

Read This

Book

Will Be

Blessed!!!!

The Book

"Despair, Hope, Salvation"

Is to Follow

Made in the USA
Columbia, SC
18 November 2020

24811918R10026